# WADDLES

## David McPhail

Abrams Books for Young Readers, New York

The illustrations in this book were made with
pen and ink and watercolor on paper.

Cataloging-in-Publication Data has been applied for
and may be obtained from the Library of Congress.
ISBN: 978-0-8109-8415-8

Printed and bound in China
10 9 8 7 6 5 4 3 2 1

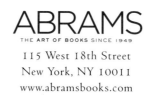

THE ART OF BOOKS SINCE 1949
115 West 18th Street
New York, NY 10011
www.abramsbooks.com

For Matthias and Josiah,
two fine brothers
— D. M.

Waddles waddled like a duck.

But he was not a duck.

Waddles was a raccoon. A very round raccoon.
And he was always hungry.

Waddles lived in a hollow tree in the park near a
beautiful pond. Every day, Waddles waddled down to the
pond to visit his best friend, Emily. Emily *was* a duck.

Sometimes they went swimming together.

Other times, Emily kept Waddles company as he searched trash cans for something to eat. Emily offered to share the bugs that she caught, but Waddles preferred half-eaten sandwiches or cake.

One morning, Waddles found Emily sitting on a newly built nest.
"Would you like to go for a swim?" Waddles asked her.
"Not today, Waddles," said Emily. "I laid my eggs. Now I have
to sit on them until they hatch."

"But how will you get food for lunch?" Waddles asked.

"I'm not sure," Emily said.

"Then I will bring you food every day," Waddles told her.

A few days later, Waddles brought Emily some breakfast.
"Oh, how I wish I could go for a swim," Emily said.
"Why don't you?" Waddles said. "I can sit on the eggs for a while."

At first, Emily hesitated, but then she thought about it. "That's a splendid idea!" she said. "You are very cuddly. And with all your soft fur, surely you will keep the eggs safe and warm."

So Emily went off for a swim.

Waddles waddled over to the nest and made himself comfortable. He felt very proud that he could help Emily and protect her eggs.

Suddenly, Waddles felt a poke. And then another.
He turned his head to see a red fox crouching behind
him. Waddles started to growl.

He knew the fox wanted to steal the eggs.
But Waddles had promised to protect the
eggs, and Waddles kept his promises.

When the fox saw how determined Waddles
was, he slowly slunk away.

Then, Waddles felt a tickle underneath him. At first he thought the fox had returned, but one by one, the eggs were beginning to hatch! Soon, five little ducklings poked their heads out of the shells and began to chirp.

"Let's go find your mother," Waddles told the ducklings. The ducklings tumbled out of their eggs and made a ragged line behind him. Together, they waddled to the pond.

Emily laughed when she saw them. "Oh, Waddles, what a lovely little family you have!" she said. And then they all had a swim.

# SUMMER

Every day, Waddles visited the ducklings. Sometimes Waddles told them stories. Sometimes they went swimming. Sometimes they shared their favorite snacks. And sometimes they all just cuddled together for a nap in the warm sun. Waddles had never been so happy.

Soon the ducklings were not little anymore.
They were nearly as big as their mother.
The days grew shorter. The wind blew colder.
The ground in the park was covered in leaves.

One morning, as Waddles waddled to the pond, he noticed the park was covered with a glimmering coat of frost. "Good morning, Waddles," Emily said. "I'm afraid it is time for us to fly south. This park will be no place for us when the winter comes."

This was the saddest news Waddles had ever heard. What would he do without Emily and the five ducklings?

"Don't be sad, Waddles," Emily said. "One day it will be spring again, and then we will return."

The ducklings crowded around Waddles and hugged him good-bye. Then, with their mother leading the way, they went scooting across the pond and rose into the sky. Even after they were gone from view, Waddles could still hear them quacking. Finally, their sounds faded, and he was alone.

WINTER

Winter had never bothered Waddles before. His thick fur kept him warm, and the park was always so beautiful in the snow. But it just wasn't the same. There was no one to tell stories to. Or to ice skate on the pond with. Or to share snacks with. Or to cuddle next to for a nap.

Waddles still looked through the trash cans
for food, but he just wasn't very hungry.

The cold days slowly passed. Then, one day,
Waddles discovered a little flower pushing up
through the melting snow.

Waddles heard a noise in the distance.
It was the sound of ducks quacking.
Many ducks! Waddles raced
to the pond—just in
time to see Emily
and the ducklings
splash down!

"Waddles!" they all cried. "We missed you!"
The ducklings, who were now grown-up ducks,
crowded around him and hugged him tight.
Winter was finally over. The ducks had come home!

The trees filled with leaves and blossoms. The sun warmed the water in the pond. Spring had returned and brought Waddles's best friends with it. Once again, snacks tasted sweet, and life in the park was as it should be. Waddles felt very full.